The House on Verdon Street

Theresa Marrama

Do you believe in ghosts?

TABLE OF CONTENTS

ACKNOWLEDGMENTS

A big **THANK YOU** to the Sarah Fitzgerald for her amazing translation of this story into English and to Valerie Dunning for her time spent editing and fine tuning this story for publication!

Prologue

Lara hears a noise. She walks toward the door. She sees that the door doesn't have a doorknob. The door is open. She thinks she hears Cheryl's voice,

"Lara, come!"

She slowly enters the room.

"Cheryl, what are you doing?" asks Lara.

Lara doesn't see Cheryl. She looks in the bedroom. It is completely black in the bedroom. She doesn't see anything. Suddenly, she hears a noise behind her. She quickly turns around. She sees the door close itself. The door quickly closes itself. She is paralyzed by fear. She is motionless. There is total silence. She doesn't hear anything. She doesn't hear anyone.

She walks toward the door. She can't open it. She starts hitting the door. She yells,

"Cheryl! Cheryl! Cheryl!"

She continues to yell, but nobody hears her.

Chapter 1

Cheryl is in her room. She's a little sad. She has a lot of memories in this house. She doesn't want to live in another house, but she doesn't want to live in this house without her dad. There are too many memories of him in this house. It's too difficult for her. She thinks of the memories when, suddenly, she hears a voice.

"Cheryl! Are you coming?"

She looks at her room again. She closes the door and with a sad voice, she yells,

"Yes, mom, I'm coming!"

A few minutes later, they are in the car. In the car, no one talks. There's a great silence. Cheryl looks out the window and she thinks. She thinks about everything. She thinks about her dad. She thinks about her life without her dad. Cheryl doesn't have any brothers or sisters. There is only her mom and her.

"Cheryl, you're not saying anything. Are you okay?" her mom asks.

Cheryl looks at her mom. She doesn't respond. She continues to look out the window of the car. Since her dad died, her mom has asked her every day, "Are you okay?" She never responds. Her mom understands that her life is

different. She understands that Cheryl is
sad.

Chapter 2

Later, Cheryl looks out the window of the car when suddenly something attracts her attention. It's a house. The house isn't small. It isn't big. It's enormous! It's the biggest house that Cheryl has ever seen. There are grand columns outside of the house. There is a staircase and two big statues in front of the house.

The car stops in front of the house.

"Mom, are you sure that it's this house?

"Yes, it's the address that the agency gave me."

"But mom, this house is enormous!"

"Yes, it's enormous, that's true!"

Cheryl continues to look at the house. She can't believe her eyes. This house is the biggest house that she has ever seen. She opens the door and gets out of the car after her mom. She looks in the direction of the statues in front of the house. The statues have a very serious expression. It seems that the statues are watching Cheryl. It seems that the eyes of the statues watch her intensely. When she looks at the house, she feels a shiver up her spine. At this moment, she hears a voice,

"Hello."

Cheryl jumps with surprise, and when she turns around, there is a woman, a very old woman.

"Ohhhh, you scared me."

She watches the old woman. The woman asks Cheryl,

"Are you here to see the house?"

Cheryl and her mom look at the house and her mom responds,

"Yes, but I think that this house is too big for my daughter and me. Maybe we can look at a smaller house?"

The old woman responds to her,

"You don't understand. This house is perfect. You're searching for a house immediately, right? Look at the house, and after if this house isn't perfect for you, we can talk."

Cheryl thinks, *"This house is too big for us. This house scares me."*

Her mom goes into the house with the old woman, but Cheryl stays in the front of the house. She observes the house. After some time, her mom returns. She looks at Cheryl and says to her,

"What do you think of the house?"

"This house scares me, Mom. I don't want to stay here"

"Oh, Cheryl. It's just a house."

Cheryl doesn't immediately respond. She looks at the house once again.

"Cheryl, this house is perfect because it is furnished. The house is not occupied, and the rent is cheap."

Cheryl rolls her eyes and says to herself, *just a house that resembles one from a horror film.*

At this moment, the old woman arrives and asks Cheryl's mom,

"What do you think? "I think that we can stay here," responds her mom.

"Excellent. I think that this house is perfect for you," says the old woman.

The old woman gives a business card to Cheryl's mom with her information. Her mom takes the business card and looks at it.

She says, "Thank you," to the old woman.

The old woman walks in the street toward her car. When the woman walks, Cheryl stays in front of the front door. She turns around to see the old woman, but she is no longer there. Cheryl sees a little girl walking on the sidewalk but not the old woman. She looks at her mom for a moment and when she turns around, the little girl is no longer there. It's as if she has disappeared also. How bizarre!

Cheryl doesn't understand the situation. She thinks, *"Maybe I'm very tired."* She turns around and she enters the house. Tonight, Cheryl and her mom are going to sleep in the enormous old house.

Chapter 3

The next day, Cheryl wakes up in her new bedroom in the old house. She gets up. Half asleep, she walks to the bathroom when something attracts her attention. She sees a painting on the wall. She examines the painting, there's a woman who looks at a little girl. The little girl looks toward the other side of the scene. The little girl has a serious expression.

At this moment, Cheryl gets shivers up her spine. Cheryl doesn't know exactly why, but the little girl in the painting attracts her attention.

A few minutes later, she goes into the kitchen. She sees her mom.

"Cheryl, we're going to the psychologist today"

"Oh, mom. I don't want to go there. Can we stay at the house today?"

"No, not today. We have to go there today, it's important!"

Cheryl returns to her room to get ready. When she opens her backpack to look for her clothes, she sees a photo of her dad. She takes the photo and looks at it. Her dad has been dead for a year. He had cancer. It was very difficult for Cheryl to see her dad like that. He had always had a lot of energy.

She starts to cry. Suddenly, she hears a noise behind her. She turns around but doesn't see anything. She continues to think of her dad looking at the photo when she hears,

"Cheryl, let's go!"

"I'm coming mom."

She puts the photo of her dad on her bed, and she quickly gets dressed. She leaves her bedroom and as she walks down the hallway, it seems that someone is watching her. She turns around and sees the painting of the woman and little girl.

What? She thinks to herself. Is the girl in this painting looking at me? She was looking in the other direction when I saw the painting this morning. Cheryl has a shiver up her spine, *"It's only my imagination,"* she thinks.

In the car, her mom asks her, "Did you sleep well?"

"Yes, but I heard a lot of noise in the house during the night." "Me too, it's an old house, it's normal."

"The house is a little weird, don't you think?" asks Cheryl

"It's just big and old. You can talk to the psychologist today, it's important for you."

A few minutes later, they arrive at the psychologist's office. After her dad's death, Cheryl and her mom had started talking with a therapist. Cheryl doesn't want to talk with the therapist, but her mom thinks that it's a good idea.

Chapter 4

After the visit to the psychologist, Cheryl is in the car with her mom when, suddenly, her phone vibrates. She looks at it and sees a text from Lara. Lara is her best friend.

> ***How are you?***
> ***And how is your new house?***

"A text?" her mom asks.

"Yes."

"From whom?" her mom asks.

"From Lara."

"Maybe she can visit us this weekend?" her mom proposes.

"Really?"

"Yes, but her mom has to drive her."

Cheryl looks at her phone and responds.

> *I am good. The house is enormous and looks like it came right out of a horror film. HAHAHA! Do you want to visit this weekend? Can your mom drive you here?*

Cheryl looks at her phone and responds.

A few minutes later her phone vibrates again.

> **YES! My mom can drive me! See you this weekend!**

"Lara can visit us this weekend. Her mom is going to drive her," says Cheryl to her mom.

"Good. Let's go to the supermarket. There is nothing to eat in the house."

At the store, the cashier, an old man, starts up a conversation with Cheryl's mom. He says,

"Hello madam. Are you visiting this village? I don't recognize you."

"No, we live in a big house, at 13 Verdon Street."

"Oh, really? The Verdon house... No one has wanted to live there since the accident."

"Huh? What accident? I think that you're talking about another house."

"No, the house is no good. It has been ten years; there was an accident with a woman and a little girl in the house. The two were found dead in the house, and everyone believes that they haunt the house now. No one wants to live there. There are weird things that happen in that house."

Cheryl hears the whole conversation. She doesn't say anything. She looks at her mom in silence. She says to herself, *Is it possible that the house is haunted? Maybe all that I see is not just in my imagination...*

After they return to the house, Cheryl goes to her bedroom to change her clothes. When she's in her room, she thinks she sees something pass by in front of the door. She turns around to look again, but she sees no one.

A few minutes later, her mom enters her bedroom.

"Cheryl, do you want to eat?"

"Yes, mom, but did you pass by the door a moment ago?"

"Huh? No."

"Oh, I think that I saw something pass by my room but…

"Oh, Cheryl. It's just your imagination."

"Mom, do you think haunted houses exist?"

"No, a house can't be haunted. It's just a rumor, Cheryl. Don't worry! This house is not haunted!

Cheryl doesn't respond. She thinks about everything that has happened. She thinks about the painting. She thinks about the noises. Her mom interrupts her thinking when she says,

"Do you want to watch a movie tonight with a big bowl of popcorn?"

"Ok, mom."

Chapter 5

Later, Cheryl watches a movie with her mom. Her mom pauses the movie to go to the bathroom. Cheryl looks at her phone on the little table in front of the couch to look at the time. It's 11:00 p.m. She gets up off the sofa and goes into the kitchen to get some more popcorn.

Moments later, she's on the couch when she hears the phone. Her mom enters the living room and answers the phone, "Hello? Hello?" There's silence. "Hello?" No one answers.

"Who is it?" Cheryl asks.

"Nobody. I heard some noise, but there was no one."

After the movie, her mom goes to the bathroom and Cheryl goes to her bedroom with the bowl of popcorn. She puts the bowl on the table next to her bed and looks for her phone. It's not there. She returns to the living room to look for it, and she hears a noise under the couch. *"That's weird,"* she thinks. She wants to look under the couch when suddenly she hears a noise. She hears a cry.

"AHHHHHH!"

This noise sends a shiver down her spine. Cheryl immediately gets up and runs to the bathroom to make sure that her mom is okay.

"Mom, Mom! Are you okay? Is there a problem?"

"Oh, the water isn't hot. I'm going to go to the basement to look at the hot water heater."

"Oh. You scared me!"

Cheryl goes into her room and her mom goes down the stairs to the basement to make sure that the hot water heater is working. A few minutes later, Cheryl is in her room when she hears,

"Cheryl! Cheryl?!"

Her mom walks into her room, panicked. She sees that Cheryl is on her bed.

"Cheryl, it's not funny!" her mom yells.

"What are you talking about Mom?"

"You closed the basement door."

"Huh? I don't understand. No, I didn't close the basement door. I was in the bedroom. I've been looking for my phone," says Cheryl seriously.

Her mom looks at her with a bizarre expression.

"Mom, it's just an old house, "says Cheryl. "I can't find my phone. I'm sure that I saw it in the living room before the movie. Have you seen it?"

"No, maybe it's on the kitchen table."

Cheryl gets up and goes to the kitchen. She doesn't see her phone. She says to herself, *how weird!*

Chapter 6

The next day Lara arrives at 1:00. When she gets out of the car, she looks at the house. She can't believe her eyes. She thinks about Cheryl's text,

"The house is enormous and looks like a house from a horror movie." The house looks exactly like a house from a horror movie. It's the biggest house that Lara has ever seen.

She walks toward the front door. She sees two statues. One statue has a serious expression. It seems that the statue is looking at her. She feels a shiver down her spine.

At this moment, she hears a noise, and she sees the front door open slowly. She jumps.

"Lara! You're here!" says Cheryl with a lot of enthusiasm.

"Cheryl, yes! You scared me!" "Come! I can show you my bedroom and the house!" Cheryl says.

For the rest of the day, the two girls talk a lot. They explore the house. When they explore, Cheryl sees a door that isn't like the others in the house.

"Lara, look at this door."

"Why? Did you find something bizarre?" Lara asks.

"The door doesn't have a doorknob. That's very weird."

The two girls look at the door in silence. Cheryl touches the door. She puts her ear against the door. Lara also puts her ear against the door.

"Do you hear that?" Lara asks.

"Yes."

"Lara, what is that noise?" Cheryl asks.

"I don't know."

Lara doesn't finish her sentence. A loud noise behind the door scares her. Cheryl looks at Lara and, at this moment, the two girls quickly run to the living room to look for Cheryl's mom.

"Mom! I'm sure that this house is haunted!"

"Huh? Cheryl.... Don't scare Lara. It's just an old house."

"I want to research the history of this house," says Cheryl.

"Cheryl, I have an idea," Lara says.

Lara grabs her phone. On the internet, she finds some information about the house. She reads to them,

Horrible Accident, 13 Verdon Street

Octobre 14, 2009

The night of Friday the 13th, there was a horrible accident at the house of 13 Verdon Street. A woman and her daughter were found dead in the house. The two were found alone. No one knows exactly how the two victims died.

"The article continues," says Lara,

According to the people who have lived in the house since the mysterious deaths, the two victims haunt the house. There is a presence in the house that no one can explain. The house was abandoned for a long time, and it's the reason why the rent today is so cheap.

Cheryl looks at her mom with big eyes.

"Mom! I'm sure that this house is haunted! Others also believe that this house is haunted!"

"Cheryl, it's just an article on the internet. No one knows if this article is true. Stop looking at the information on the phone for the night. It's late. Let's go to bed."

The two girls go to Cheryl's bedroom to sleep.

Chapter 7

After an hour, Lara still can't sleep. She slowly gets up. She looks at Cheryl and says to her,

"Cheryl, are you asleep? I can't sleep. I have to go to the bathroom."

Cheryl doesn't respond. Lara has to go to the bathroom. She slowly walks toward the door. She opens the door. She walks in the direction of the bathroom. When she gets to the bathroom, she slowly opens the door. She enters and closes it behind her.

At this moment, she hears a noise. She looks at the door. She sees something bizarre. The doorknob of the door starts to turn.

"Cheryl? Is that you?" asks Lara. No one responds.

The door continues to open itself a little. Lara jumps. She is paralyzed with fear. Finally, she says, "The bathroom is occupied."

The doorknob stops turning. She hears a noise behind the door. She looks at the door in silence for a moment. She puts her hand on the handle and opens the door slowly.

There is nobody.

She walks toward Cheryl's room, but she hears a noise. She turns around and looks behind her. She sees no one.

Lara continues to walk toward the bedroom when she sees the bedroom door is open. Suddenly, Lara hears

Cheryl's voice behind her. The voice comes from the stairs. Lara turns around and walks toward the stairs.

"Cheryl, are you there? What are you doing?" Lara murmurs.

When she is on the stairs, Lara doesn't see Cheryl, but she sees Cheryl's mom at the bottom. Lara is very scared. She is paralyzed. Cheryl's mom looks different. It's as if she were in a trance. She is in front of the front door. She isn't moving. Lara is worried and she says to her,

"Ma'am, are you okay?"

At this moment, Lara thinks that she sees a little girl pass in front of the door, at the bottom of the stairs. She closes her eyes and looks again. She is paralyzed by fear. She doesn't understand what she's seeing.

"Lara, what are you doing?"

Lara jumps and yells, terrified.

"AHHHHH! Cheryl, I heard a noise, and I saw your mom at the bottom of the stairs."

"What? My mom? My mom is asleep, Lara."

Lara looks at the bottom of the stairs again. No one is there.

"I'm sure that I saw someone at the bottom of the stairs," says Lara.

"It's just your imagination. I think that you're tired. It's 3 in the morning. You have to sleep."

Chapter 8

Later, during the night, there is a noise, a horrible noise. It's the house alarm. Cheryl immediately wakes up. She puts her hands on her ears.

Cheryl walks down the stairs. "Mom! Mom!" She cries, but her mom doesn't respond.

The alarm makes a lot of noise. Cheryl searches for the alarm when she hears another noise. It's the telephone. She is paralyzed by fear. She stays still. Finally, she slowly walks, and she stops in front of the telephone. She answers the phone,

"He... Hello?"

There is a long silence. Finally, Cheryl hears,

"Good evening. This is the house security system. Your alarm was activated. Who is on the phone?"

"Cheryl."

"Okay, Cheryl. You live at 13 Verdon Street?"

"Yes.

"Did someone break into the house?

"No, I don't think so."

"Good. Are you alone in the house?

"No."

"Are you safe?"

"Yes, I think."

"Okay, Cheryl. The police are going to arrive, but I'm going to stay on the phone with you. Are all the doors to the house and all the doors in the house closed?"

"No, not the doors in the living room."

"Okay, go into the living room and close all of them.

"Really?"

"Yes. It's important."

She slowly goes into the living room.

"Are you there?"

She sees the door and she runs to close it.

"Okay, it's done."

"Now, turn around."

She stays still.

"Why?"

"Look in the living room. You never know."

She turns around very slowly and looks.

"There is no one."

"Look closer.

She walks into the living room. She looks around the living room and at this moment, she hears a murmuring voice, "*I am in the corner. Do you see me?*"

She slowly turns around and looks in the corner. She sees something. It's the little girl. She recognizes this little girl. Why does she recognize the little girl?

How? It's... It's the little girl from the painting!

Cheryl drops the telephone, and she falls to the ground, paralyzed with fear. She closes her eyes. She opens her eyes slowly. She looks in the corner again. The little girl is no longer there.

After a moment, someone knocks on the door. Cheryl jumps. She looks. It's her mom. She wants to enter the house. Cheryl slowly gets up, walks toward the door and opens it.

"Mom, what are you doing?"

Her mom doesn't respond immediately. She comes into the house. She has terror in the eyes

"I think that I saw a little girl. It's bizarre. Very bizarre. Why did the alarm activate?"

Cheryl can't believe her ears. A LITTLE GIRL

"Mom, you think that you saw a little girl? I'm sure that..."

At this moment, the alarm stops. A moment of silence passes. Suddenly someone knocks on the door. Cheryl jumps. Her mom jumps also.

Chapter 9

There is a man at the door.

"Good evening, madam. I am Mathew, the inspector. I'm here because your alarm was activated. I have some questions to ask you. May I come in?"

Cheryl's mom opens the door, and the man enters the house. He looks at the house. He can't believe his eyes.

"This house is enormous... Okay, I have some questions. Is everyone safe?"

"Yes, we are secure."

"Why was the alarm activated?"

"I don't know"

"Hmmm... That's weird. No problem. Can I look at the alarm?"

The inspector looks at the alarm. He walks toward the front door and says,

"Everything is working normally. I'm going to leave, but if you have a problem, call the police."

"Ok. Thank you very much."

The inspector walks toward his car. Cheryl looks out the window. Her mom looks at the stairs and says to her,

"Cheryl, is Lara asleep?"

Cheryl thinks about Lara. She didn't see Lara downstairs when the inspector was in the house. She says nothing. She looks at her mom. She has terror in her eyes. She quickly runs to her bedroom. Her mom runs behind her.

Chapter 10

They look at the door. The door is closed. Cheryl thinks, *"Why is the door closed? The door wasn't closed."*

Suddenly, they hear a loud noise behind the door. Cheryl looks at her mom with big eyes. She wants to open the door. She turns the doorknob, but the door doesn't open. She looks at her mom. Her mom starts to turn the doorknob. Suddenly, the door slowly opens. Her mom jumps. Cheryl enters and looks in the bedroom. Lara isn't in the bedroom

At this moment, there is a scream, "CHERYL!" Cheryl looks at her mom.

The two run toward the scream. Cheryl sees the door that doesn't have a doorknob. She yells,

"Lara!"

"Cheryl!", yells Lara another time. Suddenly, there is a big silence. Cheryl hits the door. Her mom hits the door. Some seconds later, the door opens and... Lara runs toward Cheryl and her mom.

"Lara are you ok?" asks Cheryl.

Lara trembles with fear. She doesn't respond.

"Lara, what are you doing? Why are you in this room?" asks Cheryl nervously.

"I heard your voice in the room, and the door was open. When I went into the room, the door closed behind me."

At this moment, the two girls look at Cheryl's mom. She says to them

"I don't want to stay in this house another night."

"This house gives me the chills, mom. I don't want to stay here either."

Lara, Cheryl, and her mom quickly walk to the car. There is silence in the car. Cheryl looks at the house out the window. Her mom asks them, "Are you okay?" Lara doesn't respond. Cheryl doesn't immediately respond. Sometime later, she responds,

"I'm okay, mom."

There is another silence. After some time, Cheryl says,

"I now understand why the house was abandoned for a long time. I understand why no one wants to live there. There are weird things that happen in that house."

"Yes, there is a presence in the house that no one can explain," responds her mom.

After that night, Cheryl and her mom never return to the house on 13 Verdon Street.

Epilogue

A month later, another car arrives in front of the house on 13 Verdon Street. A girl gets out of the car. She looks at the house and she can't believe her eyes. The house is enormous. She slowly walks toward the front door, and she hears a voice. She jumps. When she turns around, she sees an old woman

"Ohhhh, you scared me," says the girl.

She observes the old woman. The woman asks,

"Are you here to see the house?"

ABOUT THE AUTHOR

Theresa Marrama is a French teacher in northern New York. She has been teaching French to middle and high school students since 2007. She is also the author of many language learner novels and has also translated a variety of Spanish comprehensible readers into French. She enjoys teaching with Comprehensible Input and writing comprehensible stories for language learners.

HER BOOKS INCLUDE:

Une Obsession dangereuse, which can be purchased at www.fluencymatters.com

HER FRENCH BOOKS ON AMAZON INCLUDE:
Une disparition mystérieuse
L'île au trésor:
Première partie: La malédiction de l'île Oak
L'île au trésor:
Deuxième partie: La découverte d'un secret
La lettre
Léo et Anton
La Maison du 13 rue Verdon
Mystère au Louvre
Perdue dans les catacombes
Les chaussettes de Tito
L'accident
Kobe - Naissance d'une légende

Kobe - Naissance d'une légende (au passé)
Le Château de Chambord : Première partie : Secrets
d'une famille
Zeinixx
La leçon de chocolat
Un secret de famille
Rhumus à Paris
Rhumus se cache à Paris
La réponse

HER SPANISH BOOKS ON AMAZON INCLUDE:
La ofrenda de Sofía
Una desaparición misteriosa
Luis y Antonio
La Carta
La casa en la calle Verdón
La isla del tesoro:Primera parte: La maldición de la isla
Oak
La isla del tesoro: Segunda parte: El descubrimiento de
un secreto
Misterio en el museo
Los calcetines de Naby
El accidente
Kobe - El nacimiento de una leyenda (en tiempo
presente)
Kobe - El nacimiento de una leyenda (en tiempo pasado)
La lección del chocolate
Un secreto de familia
Rhumus en Madrid
Rhumu se esconde en Madrid
La repuesta

HER GERMAN BOOKS ON AMAZON INCLUDE:
Leona und Anna
Geräusche im Wald
Der Brief
Nachts im Museum
Die Stutzen von Tito
Der Unfall
Kobe - Geburt einer Legende
Kobe - Geburt einer Legende (Past Tense)
Das Haus Nummer 13
Schokolade
Avas Tagebuch
Rhumus in Berlin
Rhumus versteckt sich in Berlin

HER ITALIAN BOOKS ON AMAZON INCLUDE:
Luigi e Antonio
I calzini di Naby
Rhumus a Roma
La lettera

HER ENGLISH BOOKS ON AMAZON INCLUDE:
Leo and Anthony
The Myesterious Disappearance
Rhumus in Paris
Mystery at the Louvre
The Chocolate Lesson
Treasure Island: Part I: The Curse of Oak Island
Treasure Island: Part II: The Discovery of a Secret
The Chambord Castle: Part I: Family Secrets

**Check out her website for more resources
and materials to accompany her books:**
www.compellinglanguagecorner.com

Check out her Digital E-Books:
www.digilangua.co

Made in the USA
Columbia, SC
12 December 2022

73559025R00041